Bad Baby

NANETTE NEWMAN
Illustrated by Andy Cooke

This edition published in 1999 by Diamond Books
77-85 Fulham Palace Road,
Hammersmith, London, W6 8JB

First published in Great Britain by William Collins Sons & Co. Ltd 1988
First published in Picture Lions 1990
Picture Lions is an imprint of the Children's Division, part of Harper Collins Publishers Limited
77-85 Fulham Palace Road, Hammersmith
London W6 8JB

ISBN 0 261 67371 8

Printed and bound in Singapore by Tien Wah Press
This book is set in Souvenir

Whenever Bad Baby comes over for tea everyone sighs, "Oh Dearie Me!"

She'll break all the cups.
She'll spit on the floor.

She'll crawl in the cupboards
and write on the door.

She'll yell for more biscuit
when she's given cake.

She'll comb Nana's hair
with the old garden rake.

She'll growl at the cat
and hide Daddy's money.

She'll smack "dearest Teddy"
and think it's all funny.

She'll butter her hair
and screw up her nose.

She'll snort like a pig
and bite "good baby's" toes.

She'll snatch all the toys
and twist Aunt Bessie's ear.

She'll dribble and gobble
and snarl and then sneer.

And after all that –

as if that's not enough –

She'll get out the paint box

and paint Archie's cuff!

She'll climb in the dustbin
and give it a lick.

She'll swallow some paper
and then be quite sick.

She's *always* so naughty!
She *just can't* be good!

And *nobody* likes her
(though we *wish* we could)!

She *never* says please,
she just grabs and says "More!"

She tips bowls on her head
and throws jam on the floor.

She unwinds the knitting
and tears all the books.

She screams when she's sitting
and gives nasty looks.

And then when it's time for her to go home
she stamps up and down and lets out a long moan.

We all say Goodbye
but she won't wave her hand –
She's filling the sugar bowl up
with some sand.

So whenever Bad Baby
comes over to tea
you can see why we all cry out,
"Oh Dearie Me!"

She's horrid and nasty and bad through and through.
And we're glad that we've got

A "Good Baby"
like you.